Every new generation of children is enthralled by the famous stories in our Well-loved Tales series. Younger ones love to have the story read to them. Older children will enjoy the exciting stories in an easy-to-read text.

British Library Cataloguing in Publication Data
Southgate, Vera
    The sly fox and the little red hen.—Rev. ed.—
    (Well-loved tales. Series 606D; v. 13)
    I. Title   II. Price Thomas, Brian   III. Series
    823'.914[J]   PZ7
    ISBN 0-7214-0950-4

Revised edition

Published by Ladybird Books Ltd Loughborough Leicestershire UK
Ladybird Books Inc Lewiston Maine 04240 USA

The Sly Fox
and the
Little Red Hen

retold for easy reading
by VERA SOUTHGATE M A B Com
illustrated by BRIAN PRICE THOMAS

Ladybird Books

Once upon a time there was a little red hen. She lived all by herself, in a little house in the woods.

Near the little red hen, there lived a sly young fox. He did not live by himself. He lived with his mother, in a den.

The sly young fox wanted to eat
the little red hen for his dinner.

He made all sorts of plans to catch
her. He tried many, many times to
catch her.

But she was a wise little hen. Not one of the sly fox's plans worked. He grew quite thin, trying to catch the little red hen.

One day the sly young fox said to
his mother, "Today I will catch the
little red hen. I have made the best
plan of all."

He picked up a bag and slung it
over his back.

"I shall put the little red hen in
this bag," he said to his mother as
he went out.

"Put a pot of water on the fire, to boil," he went on. "We shall have the little red hen for our dinner."

Then the sly young fox crept up to the little red hen's house. He hid himself by the side of the house and waited.

Soon the little red hen came out of her little house. She did not see the sly young fox.

She began to pick up sticks for her fire.

The little red hen had left the door of the house open.

When her back was turned, the sly young fox crept inside the house.

The sly fox hid behind the door.

The little red hen carried her wood
into the house. She shut the door.
Then she saw the sly young fox.

Poor little red hen was very frightened.

She dropped her wood. Then,
before the fox could move, she
flew up to a high beam.

Up on the high beam, the little red hen felt safe. She knew that the sly young fox could not get up there.

"Ha-ha! You can't catch me, Mr Fox," she said. "You had better go home."

"Oh! So I can't catch you!" said
the sly young fox. "We'll soon see
about that."

Then the sly young fox began to
chase his tail.

The little red hen looked down
from her beam and watched him.

Round and round went the sly
young fox, round and round
without stopping.

Soon the little red hen's head
began to go round and round,
round and round.

She became so dizzy that she fell
down from the high beam.

"Ha-ha!" said the sly young fox,
as the little red hen dropped into
his bag. "Who said I could not
catch you?"

The sly young fox slung his bag over his back and set off for his den.

On the way, the fox sat down for a rest. It was a hot day and soon he fell asleep.

38

When the fox was asleep, the little
red hen popped her head out of the
bag. Then she crept quietly out.

The little red hen then picked up
some big stones. She put the stones
into the bag. Then back home she
ran.

When the sly young fox awoke, he did not know what had happened.

He picked up his bag and set off for his den. "Dear me!" he said to himself, "this bag is becoming heavier."

As the sly young fox came to his
den, he shouted to his mother,
"I've got the little red hen, at last!
Is the water boiling?"

"Yes, my son," said his mother.

Then the sly young fox opened
the bag, over the pot of boiling
water. The big stones fell into
the water with a very big splash.

The boiling water splashed all over
the sly young fox and his mother.

They were both killed at once.

Then the little red hen lived happily ever after, in her little house in the woods.